Barbie™

Princess Tales

THE ESSENTIAL GUIDE

Barbie™

Princess Tales

THE ESSENTIAL GUIDE

DK

Contents

Welcome!

BEING A PRINCESS is much tougher than you think. It's not just a life of magic, romance, and fun—a princess must also be kind and good and brave. Enter the fairy-tale world of Barbie™ Princess Tales and share the adventures of some fabulous princesses.

Sugar Plum Island

Sea of Storms

Lush Valley

Floating stepping stones

Forest

Ice cave

The Nutcracker

Once upon a time the Land of Candy was ruled by a kind old king. When he died, his advisor, a mouse, took charge until his son, Prince Eric, could prove himself worthy of the throne. However, the mouse decided that he liked being king, so he turned the prince into a nutcracker. The mouse threatened to use his magic on anyone who disobeyed him. One day, a visitor brought hope to the Land of Candy...

Palace of Sweets

Barren Valley

Floating island

Treetop Village

Gingerbread Village

Clara's Adventure

CLARA IS A YOUNG GIRL who lives with her grandfather and younger brother, Tommy. She longs for adventure and dreams of traveling the world and visiting exotic places. But her grandfather thinks she is too young and that she belongs at home with her family.

Dreams come to life

A special Christmas gift is about to change Clara's life. When Aunt Elizabeth Drosselmeyer gives Clara a nutcracker, Clara is delighted, but Tommy wants it for himself! As he tries to snatch it from Clara, the nutcracker breaks.

Clara loves her grandfather but she feels all grown up and ready to explore the big, wide world.

Clara's Aunt Elizabeth leads a truly adventurous life. On her recent trip to Asia she met an Emperor, sailed in a junk, took a rickshaw ride, and hiked the Great Wall of China. Clara longs to travel with her.

On the stroke of midnight, the Mouse King and his army come through a knot hole in the base board. As the nutcracker comes to life, the parlor is turned into a miniature battlefield.

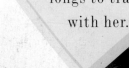

Clara thinks she must be dreaming! She tries to help Nutcracker, but the Mouse King shrinks her with a magic spell.

Wise old owl

The adventure begins

Clara bravely saves Nutcracker by throwing her slipper at the Mouse King. Unfortunately, her problems are only just beginning. The only person who can return her to her normal size is the Sugar Plum Princess, and no one knows who or where she is!

Clara and Nutcracker step through the knot hole into the magical land beyond. They land in an ice cave where snow faeries dance and the snow isn't even cold!

When Clara mends the littlest snow faerie's wing, the other faeries perform a beautiful dance to thank her. They reveal the exit to the cave.

Antique lace bodice and cuffs

Nutcracker

Clara's nutcracker is in the shape of a soldier.

Purple silk party dress

The Land of Candy

PARTHENIA OR THE LAND OF CANDY was once a happy place, but the Mouse King has spread fear throughout the land. He will not rest until he has destroyed everything that is good. Only the Sugar Plum Princess can stop him, and help Clara return to her normal size.

The Gingerbread Village

Clara is amazed by what she sees in Parthenia. The trees smell like peppermint and the village is made of gingerbread! However, the village has been ransacked and seems to be deserted.

The Peppermint Girl and Gingerbread Boy blame Prince Eric for Parthenia's problems.

Pimm is the Mouse King's spy. He knows his master will be interested in Parthenia's visitors.

Clara and Nutcracker reunite the children with the villagers who are hiding in the forest. Major Mint and Captain Candy are trying to find a way to defeat the Mouse King, so they agree to join the quest for the Sugar Plum Princess.

The Sea of Storms

Thanks to Pimm, the Mouse King is always one step ahead, and he sends a rock giant to kill Nutcracker. But Clara has helped Nutcracker believe in himself, so he is more than a match for the giant.

High up in the trees, Clara and Nutcracker grow closer as Clara guesses his true identity—Prince Eric. Clara is not sure that she wants to go home if it means leaving Nutcracker behind.

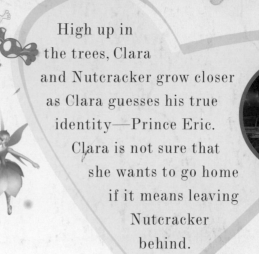

The Barren Valley used to be lush and beautiful before the Mouse King's reign. When Nutcracker and Clara release the faeries, the valley comes to life again.

Clara's Secret

THE SEARCH FOR THE Sugar Plum Princess leads Clara and her new friends to an island in the Sea of Storms. But once again the Mouse King is one step ahead, thanks to Pimm. Nutcracker, Major Mint, and Captain Candy walk straight into a trap, leaving Clara behind.

Clara to the rescue

Left alone on the island, Clara knows she could use her locket to return home, but she decides that she can't abandon Nutcracker and her friends. Luckily, the faeries she rescued in the Barren Valley arrive to repay the favor.

Clara uses her instincts to find Nutcracker when she can't see him!

The prince fights back

Nutcracker realizes that he must face the Mouse King, even without the Sugar Plum Princess. Nutcracker intends to show the Mouse King that the people of Parthenia won't be pushed around!

The Mouse King has built a big bonfire, but Nutcracker doesn't intend to be firewood!

The people of Parthenia try to stand up to the Mouse King, but he turns them to stone.

The Mouse King gets what he deserves when his own spell rebounds on him!

Royal crown

Clara's locket

Sequined bodice in a snowflake pattern

Sparkly tulle tutu

Pink satin ballet slippers

The Sugar Plum Princess

At last, Nutcracker defeats the Mouse King and the Land of Candy is free once more. Color, beauty, and happiness can return to Parthenia. And guess what? The Sugar Plum Princess was right there all along!

Clara's kiss breaks the Mouse King's spell and transforms Nutcracker back into Prince Eric. Then Clara discovers who she really is—the Sugar Plum Princess!

At last, Prince Eric has proved that he is worthy to be king, and Clara has discovered that bravery and kindness can achieve anything.

The Mouse King's final act of wickedness sends Clara back home. She is devastated to leave Prince Eric, but somehow true love always finds a way.

Magic prevents people from finding Gothel's house

Gothel's bedroom

Rapunzel

Long, long ago in a time of magic and dragons, a kind and sweet girl lived in a dark, magical forest. The girl's name was Rapunzel, and she had beautiful golden hair that was so long it reached the floor. Rapunzel was treated like a servant by her guardian, Gothel, but one magical day, a chance discovery would turn Rapunzel's world upside down.

Magic painting

The kitchen

Secret staircase

Tea service

Rapunzel's bedroom

The tower

The secret room

Silver hairbrush

Secret tunnel leading
to the village

Rapunzel's Life

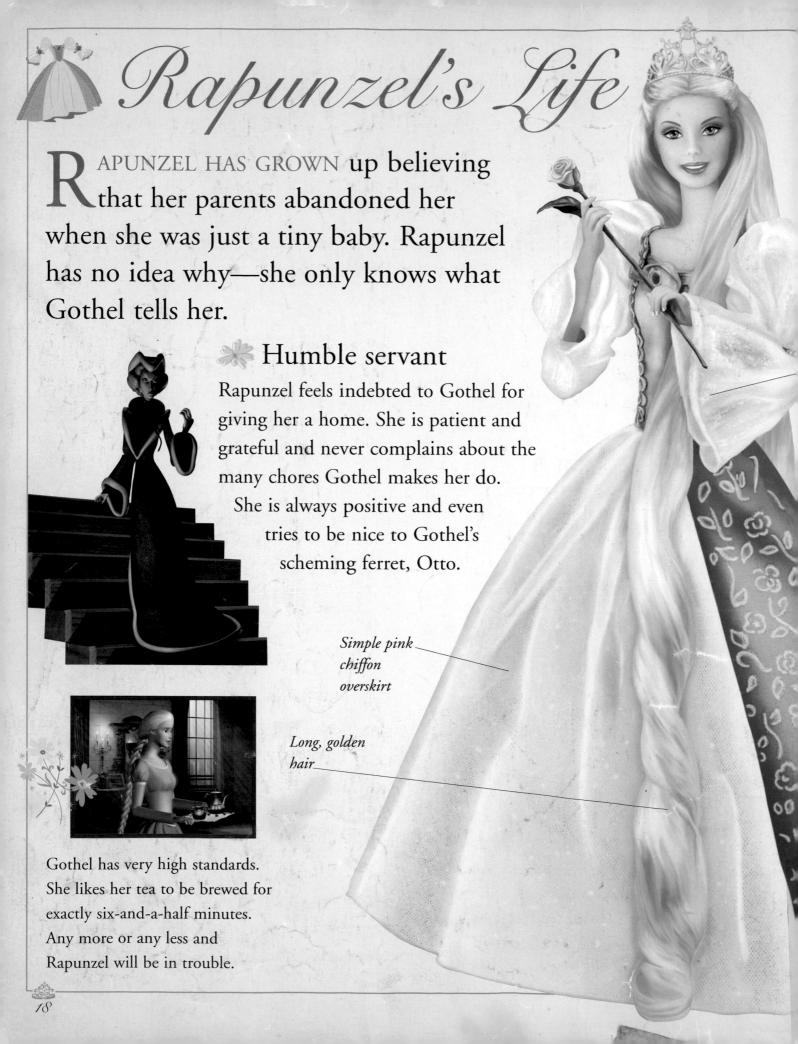

RAPUNZEL HAS GROWN up believing that her parents abandoned her when she was just a tiny baby. Rapunzel has no idea why—she only knows what Gothel tells her.

✾ Humble servant

Rapunzel feels indebted to Gothel for giving her a home. She is patient and grateful and never complains about the many chores Gothel makes her do. She is always positive and even tries to be nice to Gothel's scheming ferret, Otto.

Simple pink chiffon overskirt

Long, golden hair

Gothel has very high standards. She likes her tea to be brewed for exactly six-and-a-half minutes. Any more or any less and Rapunzel will be in trouble.

✿ Special gifts

Gothel has no idea that Rapunzel has a few good things in her life. She loves to paint—her favorite paintings are beautiful landscapes of the places she longs to visit. She has two special friends, Penelope and Hobie, who make her smile and are always on her side.

Organza sleeves, woven with shimmery thread

The inscription on the silver hairbrush reads, "Constant as the stars above, always know that you are loved. To our daughter, Rapunzel, on her first birthday. With love forever, Mother and Father."

Penelope is a clumsy young dragon. She worries that she will never be a mighty dragon like her father Hugo, who also serves Gothel.

Hobie is a crotchety rabbit with an insatiable appetite, especially for carrots! He is very loyal to Rapunzel!

Embroidered panel

The three friends find a tunnel underneath the secret room. While Hobie and Penelope stand guard, brave Rapunzel can't wait to find out where it leads!

✿ A new beginning?

Penelope's clumsiness brings about a wonderful discovery. A hidden stairway leads to a secret room underneath the kitchen. In a wooden box, Rapunzel finds a beautiful silver hairbrush and uncovers a secret that Gothel has been keeping from her.

A Different World

ALL HER LIFE, RAPUNZEL has been kept hidden from the world. She has no idea what lies beyond Gothel's house, but she can't wait to find out! While Hobie and Penelope stand guard, Rapunzel goes on an adventure that will change her life forever.

♥ The village

Rapunzel has never seen anything like this before. She is amazed by the hustle and bustle of village life—the sights and sounds, the bright colors, and the happy, smiling people. It is very different from life in the dark forest with Gothel.

While Rapunzel is walking, a little princess, Katrina, falls into a hole. Rapunzel tries to rescue Katrina, but ends up being rescued herself, by a passing handsome stranger.

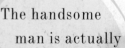

The handsome man is actually Prince Stefan, but Rapunzel doesn't know it. Stefan is dazzled by Rapunzel's beauty and her honesty. He loves it that she doesn't treat him like a prince!

Prince Stefan's little sisters Katrina, Lorena, and Melody think that Rapunzel is the most beautiful girl they have ever seen. They know she would be the perfect bride for their brother.

The secret's out!

Rapunzel can't wait to tell Penelope and Hobie all about her meeting with Stefan and the world beyond the forest. But Otto has been spying and sneaks off to tell Gothel. She demands that Rapunzel reveal the man's name.

When Rapunzel can't give her a name, Gothel thinks that she is lying and casts a spell that transforms the bedroom into a tower.

Rapunzel would never lie. She can't reveal Stefan's name to Gothel because she doesn't know it yet!

Magic paintbrush

Gothel thinks that locking Rapunzel in a tower and destroying all her paintings will keep her away from the world. But Gothel is not the only one with magic! While Rapunzel is sleeping, her silver hairbrush turns into a magical paintbrush.

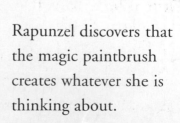

Rapunzel discovers that the magic paintbrush creates whatever she is thinking about.

The silver hairbrush reveals that Rapunzel's parents loved her. She sets off with Stefan to learn more from the man who made it.

Happy Ever After

RAPUNZEL AND STEFAN fall even more deeply in love when they meet again. Stefan invites Rapunzel to a masquerade ball. It is in honor of the prince's birthday, but she still has no idea that he is really the prince!

A royal ball

Rapunzel can't wait to go to the ball, but she needs an outfit! While Hobie and Penelope offer fashion advice, she uses her magic paintbrush to create the perfect dress. But once again, Otto ruins everything! He steals the invitation and takes it straight to Gothel.

Gothel is furious! She plans to take Rapunzel's place at the ball.

Gothel cuts off Rapunzel's beautiful golden hair. She imprisons Rapunzel in the tower and goes to the palace in disguise, to trap Stefan.

Gothel's revenge

It turns out that Gothel is worse than everyone thought! Years ago she was rejected by King Wilhelm, so she took revenge by stealing his baby daughter, Rapunzel. Wilhelm blamed his neighbor, King Frederick, and the two kings have been enemies ever since. Gothel hopes the two kings will destroy each other's kingdoms.

A true princess

Gothel's spell cannot trap Rapunzel in the tower because she has a true heart. Rapunzel no longer feels indebted to Gothel, so with Penelope and Hobie's help, she puts her in a place where she can never harm anyone ever again!

King Wilhelm is overjoyed to be reunited with his long-lost daughter. He is also glad that his feud with King Frederick is over.

Gothel gets what she deserves! She is trapped in the tower, by her own unbreakable spell. Best of all, Otto has to wait on her, just like Rapunzel used to.

At last, Rapunzel and Stefan are free to be together in peace and love. Rapunzel couldn't have painted a happier ending!

Entrance to Enchanted
Forest from village

Stepping stones

The Ancient Tree

Moonlight
picnic area

Magic Crystal

The Magic Meadow

Swan Lake

In a quiet village there lived a sweet young girl named Odette. She was very shy and was happiest at home with her father and sister, Marie. While Marie loved to ride her horse and have adventures, Odette was too timid to go with her. But one day a magical visitor led Odette on an amazing adventure, and she discovered that she was braver than she thought.

Rothbart's house

Erasmus' cave

Giant toadstools

Good Triumphs

W**HEN** E**RASMUS** reveals Rothbart's wicked plan to Odette, she is determined to stop him. There is no way she is going to let him become king of the Enchanted Forest, and there is certainly no way that she is going to let Daniel marry the wrong girl!

The royal ball

Odette is too late! Rothbart's magic has tricked Daniel into believing that Odile is his beloved Odette. When Daniel mistakenly declares his love for Odile, it looks like Rothbart has won.

Odette falls into a swoon when she hears Daniel pledge true love to the disguised Odile.

Rothbart wins?

Rothbart feels triumphant. The crystal is powerless; at last he can become king of the Enchanted Forest. The only thing he has left to do is destroy Prince Daniel.

The Fairy Queen's magic has finally run out, and Rothbart turns her into a mouse!

Odette wakes up just as Rothbart is about to strike Daniel with his magic. She rushes to save him, and at the same time Daniel tries to protect her. They are both hit and fall down together.

Overskirt made of delicate feathers

Elegant choker-style necklace

♥♥ True love

As Odette and Daniel lie on the ground, the magic crystal starts to glow. By risking their lives for each other, Odette and Daniel have proved that their love is true. Together they have defeated Rothbart and saved the Enchanted Forest.

The forest blooms brighter than ever and at last the fairy folk can break free from Rothbart's wicked spells. It is a wonderful day!

Daniel can now declare his love to the real Odette. When her family arrives, Odette's happiness is complete.

Skirt shimmering with magic

Odile and Rothbart get just what they deserve— Odile has to dust Erasmus' books, while Rothbart finds a useful way to spend his time!

The Princess and the Pauper

Long ago and far away
something amazing ocurred.
At the same time, two identical
baby girls were born. One was
born a princess and lived in a
castle surrounded by fine things.
The other was born a pauper
and lived in a tiny cottage with
no luxuries. The girls grew up
in their different worlds until a
special day came that would
change their lives forever.

The Wishing Well

The village square

Madame Carp's dress shop

Madame Carp's workshop

ANNELIESE LOVES HAVING lots of beautiful dresses and going to balls and parties. But for her, being a princess also means doing what other people want all the time. Sometimes Anneliese longs to be free to do whatever she wants, just like a regular girl.

Castle life

Princess Anneliese lives a privileged life, with all the fine things a girl could possibly want. Her days are spent doing her royal duty—smiling politely, giving speeches, being the guest of honor, and learning how to be a gracious princess.

Long, golden hair

Satin skirt overlaid with shimmering pink chiffon

Anneliese's luxurious bedroom has a queen-size bed with a silk canopy, and her closet covers a whole wall!

Gold-digger! "Loyal" servant Preminger has been secretly robbing the royal mine for years. The gold has finally run out, and he plots to marry Anneliese and become king.

Gold crown

Heart-shaped
locket with large
solitaire diamond

Satin bodice
with gold trim
and embroidery

Princess Anneliese is
secretly in love with her
tutor, Julian, but it is her
duty to marry King
Dominick and save
the kingdom.

Secret dreams

Anneliese loves studying!
Her favorite subjects are
math and science, and if
she had the choice, she
would spend all day in the library. Little
does Anneliese know that being smart
might actually save her kingdom!

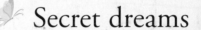

The queen wishes that there
were another way of saving
the kingdom, but marrying
Anneliese to King Dominick
is the only option.

Serafina is not just Anneliese's
beautiful pet, she is her best
friend. When Anneliese is in
danger, Serafina does
anything she can to help
her—even if it means
getting dirty.

Erika's World

ERIKA WORKS HARD day and night making beautiful dresses for other girls to wear to balls and parties. Although she never complains, Erika would love to be able to have fun and do what she wants. But like Anneliese, Erika is not free to follow her dreams.

A pauper's life

Erika must work in Madame Carp's dress shop until she has paid off her parents' debts. But the sneaky seamstress keeps adding on extra "interest" so Erika will never be free.

Erika doesn't have time for a social life, so her best friend is her cat, Wolfie. But Wolfie is not a regular cat—he barks like a dog and loves to play catch.

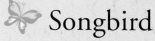

Songbird

Erika loves singing because it is the only time she can truly be free. She dreams of being a famous singer and traveling all around the world.

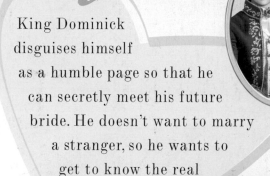

King Dominick disguises himself as a humble page so that he can secretly meet his future bride. He doesn't want to marry a stranger, so he wants to get to know the real Anneliese!

King Dominick is just about to reveal his true identity when hears Erika singing in the bathtub. He immediately falls in love with her—the only problem is, he thinks she is Princess Anneliese!

Good friend

When Erika realizes that Anneliese is in danger, she wants to help her. With the aid of *The Princess Book of Etiquette*, a blonde wig, Anneliese's fabulous clothes, and a little help from Julian, Erika is all set to take Anneliese's place and expose Preminger's plan.

Friends Forever

EVERY GIRL NEEDS A best friend, someone who knows you better than anyone else. You can tell her your secrets, share your special times, and best of all, she is always there for you when you need her. Anneliese and Erika were both alone. Until now.

 ## A girl like me

When Anneliese hears Erika singing, she follows the beautiful sound and makes an amazing discovery that will change both girls' lives forever. They look identical—except for their hair color, and the crown-shaped birthmark on Anneliese's left shoulder.

While Erika is enjoying a princess's life at the royal palace, Anneliese finds out what it's like to be a pauper—a lot of hard work!

It was love at first sight for Wolfie and Serafina. Anneliese and Erika think that their pets make a purrfect couple!

Friends in need

Preminger seems to have won: Erika is in the dungeon, and everyone believes that Anneliese has perished in the mine. Luckily, Anneliese and Erika will not give up without a fight!

Just as Preminger is about to marry the queen and become king, Anneliese and Erika arrive to spoil his party. It's about time he got his just desserts!

Happily ever after

Now that the kingdom and her mother have been saved, Anneliese is free to be with Julian. Erika, too, can finally follow her dreams and become a famous singer. However, she realizes that fame and glory are nothing without love, and she returns home to share a special double wedding day with her best friend.

In a far away kingdom, an
evil wizard called Wenlock
decided to marry the most
beautiful girl in the
kingdom—Princess Brietta.
When she refused, he turned
her into a flying horse!
Princess Brietta sought
safety in the Cloud Kingdom,
while her parents, the king
and queen, did everything
they could to protect their other
daughter, Annika, from harm.
One day, Wenlock decides it is
time to find a new wife...

Annika's Journey

MOST PEOPLE THINK the Wand of Light is a myth, but Annika believes that it is real, and she is determined to build one and save her parents. All she needs is a Measure of Courage, a Ring of Love, and a Gem of Ice lit by Hope's Eternal Flame.

The Wand of Light

Annika sets out on her quest with Aidan, Brietta, and Shiver. She finds a Measure of Courage in the ribbon she uses to outsmart a scary giant, and a Gem of Ice is a diamond sparkling in the dawn sunlight.

All Annika needs is the Ring of Love, and Aidan hopes he can make one. Brietta offers her royal crown instead.

Brietta's crown is the Ring of Love! It completes the Wand of Light, and Aidan forges the pieces together.

Brietta transformed

Annika uses the Wand of Light to turn Brietta back into a human. It works! But Wenlock arrives to ruin everything. Annika tries to use the wand on Wenlock, but nothing happens! He takes the wand and traps Annika in the ice.

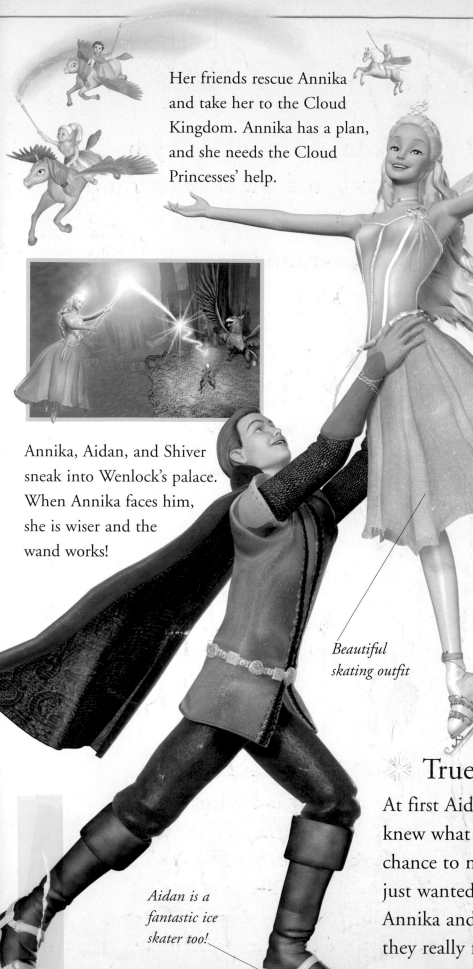

Her friends rescue Annika and take her to the Cloud Kingdom. Annika has a plan, and she needs the Cloud Princesses' help.

Every day the Cloud Princesses paint the sunrise and sunset across the sky. Today, to give Annika extra time to save her parents and her people, the Princesses paint the sunset very slowly.

Annika is happiest when she is skating—with Aidan!

Annika, Aidan, and Shiver sneak into Wenlock's palace. When Annika faces him, she is wiser and the wand works!

Beautiful skating outfit

The Cloud Queen is delighted that Wenlock has been defeated, but she will miss Brietta.

True feelings revealed

At first Aidan helped Annika because he knew what it was like to want a second chance to make things right, but later, he just wanted to to be with her. At last, Annika and Aidan tell each other what they really feel—it's true love!

Aidan is a fantastic ice skater too!

45

The Happy Ending

THE ONLY SURE THING in the magical world of fairy tales is that everything will turn out right in the end. But each princess has to learn a very important lesson before she reaches her happy ending.

The Nutcracker
On her adventure, Clara discovers that if you are kind, clever, and brave, anything is possible.

Swan Lake
Odette learns that she is braver than she thought, and she discovers the power of true and selfless love.

Rapunzel
With love and imagination, Rapunzel is able to change her life and the lives of the people she loves.

The Princess and the Pauper
Every person has a unique gift—whether it is science or singing—and in that gift lies their destiny. Together Anneliese and Erika learn how to live their dreams.

The Magic of Pegasus
Annika discovers that with courage, determination, and love, she can achieve anything!

DK

LONDON, NEW YORK, MUNICH,
MELBOURNE, AND DELHI

Project Editor Catherine Saunders
Designer Lisa Crowe
Publishing Manager Simon Beecroft
Category Publisher Alex Allan
Art Director Mark Richards
Production Claire Pearson
DTP Designer Lauren Egan

First American Edition, 2005
Published in the United States by

DK Publishing, Inc.
375 Hudson Street
New York, New York 10014

ISBN 0-7566-1333-7

Color reproduction by Media Development and
Printing Ltd., UK

Printed and bound in China by SNP Leefung Printers Ltd.

Acknowledgments

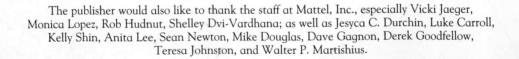

Based on the original screenplays by Clif Ruby & Elana Lesser

The publisher would also like to thank the staff at Mattel, Inc., especially Vicki Jaeger,
Monica Lopez, Rob Hudnut, Shelley Dvi-Vardhana; as well as Jesyca C. Durchin, Luke Carroll,
Kelly Shin, Anita Lee, Sean Newton, Mike Douglas, Dave Gagnon, Derek Goodfellow,
Teresa Johnston, and Walter P. Martishius.

Discover more at
www.dk.com